anythink

Digger and Daisy
Go to the Zoo

By Judy Young
Illustrated by
Dana Sullivan

Text Copyright © 2013 Judy Young
Illustration Copyright © 2013 Dana Sullivan

Sleeping Bear Press™

315 E. Eisenhower Parkway, Ste. 200
Ann Arbor, MI 48108
www.sleepingbearpress.com

Printed and bound in the United States.

10 9 8 7 6 5 4 3 2 1 (case)
10 9 8 7 6 5 4 3 2 1 (pbk))

Library of Congress Cataloging-in-Publication Data

Young, Judy.
Digger and Daisy go to the zoo / written by Judy Young;
illustrated by Dana Sullivan.
pages cm
Summary: When Digger the dog and his big sister Daisy visit the zoo,
Digger tries to imitate the animals they see and Daisy tells him that although
he cannot climb a tree like a monkey, he can swim in a pond like a duck.
ISBN 978-1-58536-841-9 (hard cover) — ISBN 978-1-58536-842-6 (paper back)
[1. Ability—Fiction. 2. Zoo animals—Fiction. 3. Brothers and sisters—Fiction.
4. Dogs—Fiction.] I. Sullivan, Dana, illustrator. II. Title.
PZ7.Y8664Dig 2013
[E]—dc23
2013004090

For Jordan
—Judy

To Kyle, who smells like a monkey.
—Dana

It is a hot day.

"Do you want to go to the zoo?"
says Daisy.

"Yes," says Digger.

"I like the zoo."

Digger and Daisy look at birds.

They see big birds.

They see little birds.

Red birds. Green birds.

Yellow and blue birds, too.

"Look at that bird," says Daisy.

Digger looks at the bird.

It is pink.

It stands on one leg.

"I want to stand like that bird,"
Digger says.

Digger tries to stand on one leg.

He wiggles.
He wobbles.

And over
he falls.

Daisy laughs.

"We cannot stand on one leg,"
she says.

"We will fall over.

But we can walk on two legs."

Daisy and Digger walk on two
legs.
They walk over to the monkeys.

A monkey is in a tree.

"I want to climb a tree," says Digger.

Digger tries to climb a tree.

He cannot.

Daisy laughs.

"We cannot climb trees," Daisy says. "But we can climb stairs."

Daisy and Digger climb stairs.

They go up and up.

Soon they are as high as the giraffe.

The giraffe eats a leaf from a tree.

Digger wants
to eat a leaf
from a tree.

Daisy laughs.
"We cannot eat a leaf from a
tree," she says.

"I need a drink now," says Digger.

"Can we get a drink?"

"Yes," says Daisy.

"Cold water is good on a hot day."

"I see more water," says Digger.

"Can we go there?"

"Yes," says Daisy.

A duck swims in the water.

"I want to swim," says Digger.

"Can I swim?"

Daisy laughs.

"Yes," she says. "You can swim."

Digger puts one leg in the water.

"Am I swimming?" says Digger.

"No, you are not swimming,"

Daisy says.

Digger puts two legs in the water.

"Am I swimming now?" says

Digger.

"No, you are not swimming,"

Daisy says.

"You must jump in all the way."

Digger is not sure.

"I cannot stand on one leg," Digger says.

"I cannot climb a tree.
And I cannot eat a leaf from a tree."

"Are you sure I can swim?"

"Yes," says Daisy.

"You can swim. Just try."

Digger takes a breath.

He closes his eyes.

And he jumps!

Into the water goes Digger.

He splishes.

He splashes.

He swims!

Digger swims in the water.

He swims by the duck.

"I am swimming," he says to the duck.

Digger swims by a frog.

"I am swimming," he says to the
frog.

Digger swims by Daisy.

"I am swimming," he says to Daisy.

"Come on in. The water is nice!"

Daisy goes into the water.

"The water is cold," says Daisy.

"Stand on one leg," says Digger.

Daisy stands on one leg.

She wiggles. She wobbles.

Splash! Daisy falls in!

Digger laughs.

"We cannot stand on one leg,"
says Digger.
"But you said cold water is good
on a hot day."